Black Dancers
ALL AGES COLORING BOOK

BY: A.C. WASHINGTON

ILLUSTRATIONS BY:
ROXY HANA
ELISA SECCA
JULIA MOOLEN
JODELYN C. PAET

Black Dancers

ALL AGES COLORING BOOK

Copyright © 2021 by A.C. Washington

No part of this book may be used or reproduced in any manner whatsoever without the prior written permission of the author.

ISBN: 9781735069791

Find more info at scruffypuppress.com

This Book Belongs To:

I love the way my body moves

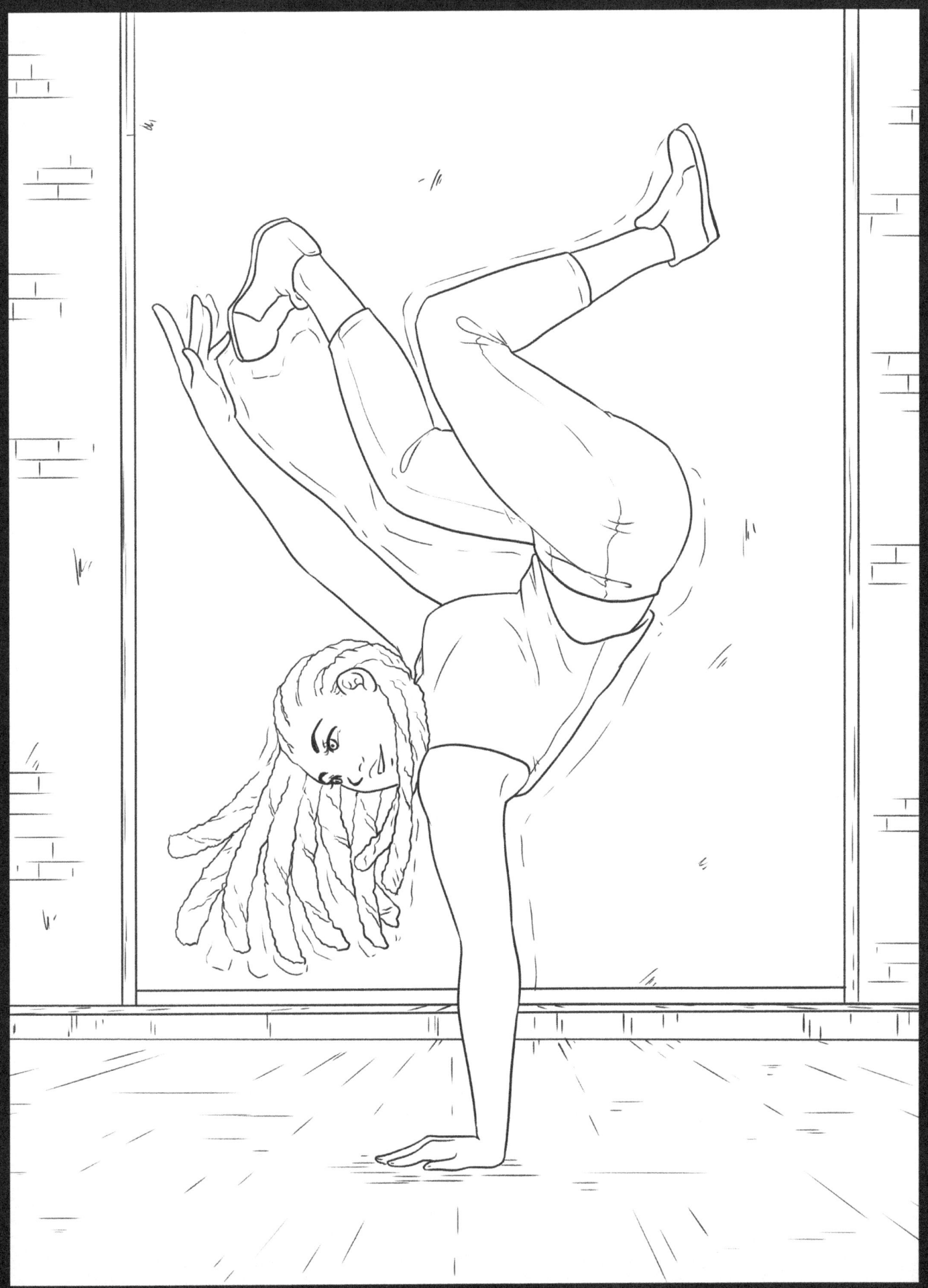

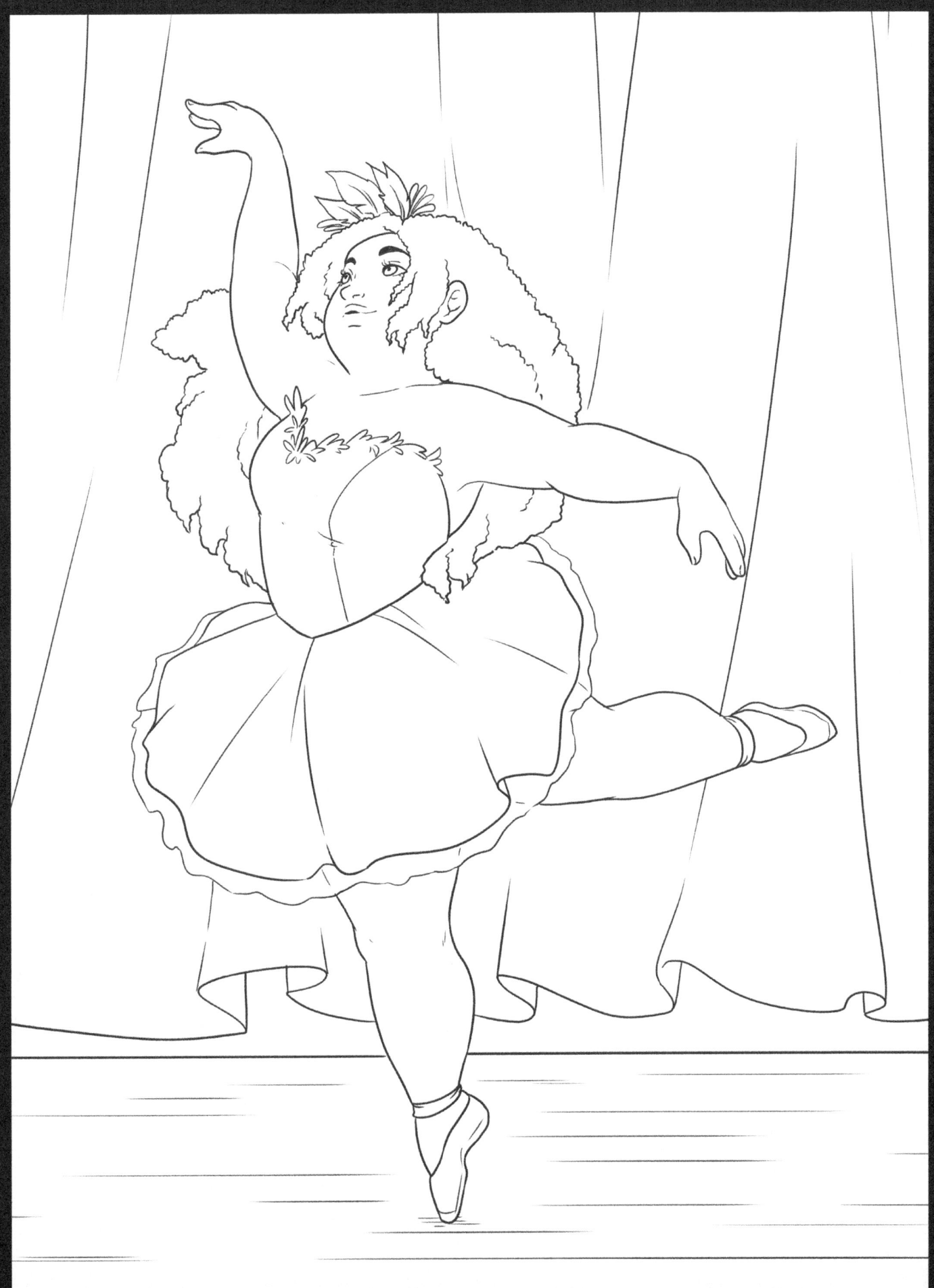

DANCE TO YOUR OWN RHYTHM

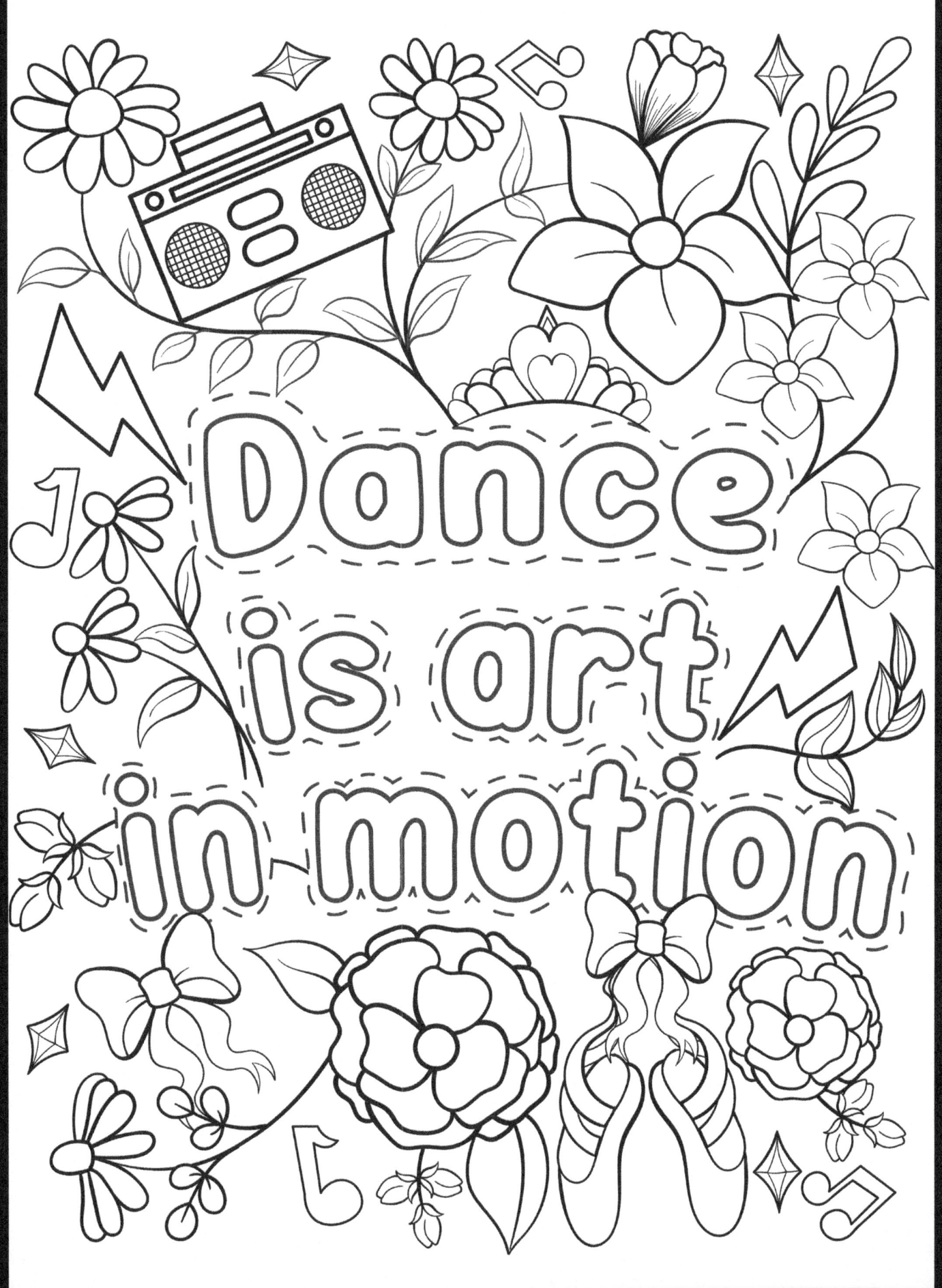

Thank you for your purchase!

Find more books at ScruffyPupPress.com.

If you enjoyed this coloring experience, please leave a review on Amazon!

Scruffy Pup Press

Made in the USA
Monee, IL
19 April 2023

www.mascotbooks.com

One Grillie

©2023 Sandy Reitman. All Rights Reserved. No part of this publication may be reproduced, stored in a retrieval system or transmitted in any form by any means electronic, mechanical, or photocopying, recording or otherwise without the permission of the author.

For more information, please contact:
Mascot Kids, an imprint of Amplify Publishing Group
620 Herndon Parkway, Suite 320
Herndon, VA 20170
info@mascotbooks.com

Library of Congress Control Number: 2022903074

CPSIA Code: PRT0622A

ISBN-13: 978-1-63755-400-5

Printed in the United States

To my mom, Martha,
with much love.

All Grilled Cheeses start out the same—two fresh pieces of bread and a cold slice of cheese in the middle. Much like all the other snacks in Griddleville, Grillie was bread on the outside and cheese on the inside.

But she always felt different from everyone else and couldn't figure out what it was exactly.

There are many different types of Grilled Cheeses in Griddleville.

Some are **big**.

Some are small.

Some are made with rye bread.

Some are made with multigrain bread.

Some are gluten-free.

Some are vegan.

Some have cheddar cheese.

Some have swiss cheese.

Even though Grillie always looks like her other Grilled Cheese friends...

SHE WASN'T LIKE THEM AT *all*

While her friends were going off and meeting the perfect side dishes, taking dives into tomato soup, or jumping onto better plates, Grillie was off on her own adventure trying to discover just what it was that made her different.

She decided to leave and see what life was like beyond Griddleville.

She traveled to Fryer Farm.

She went to Fridge City.

She visited Shelfville.

And she even toured Trash Town!

Back in Griddleville, her friends were following a similar order. Should she follow that same path?

Were her adventures leading her anywhere?

She felt like she was having a bit of a meltdown.

One day, she had had enough of being a to-go Grillie, so she packed up her things and returned home.

Once Grillie was back in Griddleville, she sat down with Mama Grill. She asked, "Why do I feel so different from every other Grilled Cheese in Griddleville?"

Mama Grill turned and looked at her with loving eyes. "We put a special blend of cheeses in you when you were born. One that would never settle for anything less than the extraordinary. You are filled with a combination of all cheeses, and you can be whoever you want!"

It was then that Grillie understood that she was always on her own path, and she would never doubt herself again.

One special Grillie, coming right up!

About the Author

Sandy Reitman is a professional writer based in Milwaukee, Wisconsin. Her day job has her writing website copy and corporate communications, but she finds her true passion in creative writing. *One Grillie* is her first adventure into the wonderful world of children's books, and she plans to continue Grillie's search for herself while also continuing her own quest for meaning.

About the Illustrator

Amelina Jones is an illustrator with a passion for nature, tea, and stories. She works in traditional watercolor and ink, incorporating storytelling elements and emotions into her work. The gentle form of watercolor mixed with her unique, whimsical style creates illustrations that aim to enhance a story and bring it to life. You can find more of AJ's work on her website, amelinajones.com, or on Instagram @amelinajonesart.